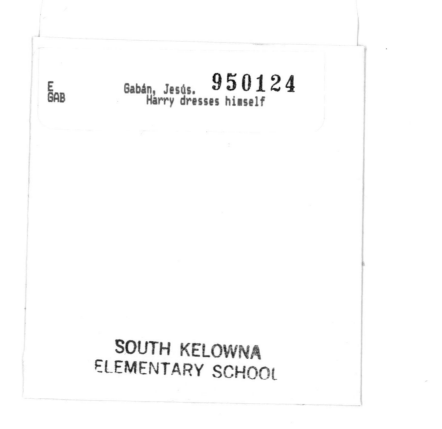

HARRY THE HIPPO

HARRY Dresses Himself

By Jesús Gabán

Gareth Stevens Children's Books
MILWAUKEE

Today, Harry decides to
get dressed by himself.

He begins with his socks.
First one foot, then the
other. "I like these colors."

3

Next, his shirt. "These
butterflies are so pretty!"

"Uh-oh! The buttons
are all mixed up!"

"Oh, well. I'll just put on
my sweater. That will
cover up the buttons."

"Look at all the pockets
on my overalls! I can put
all my treasures in them!"

"My slippers look nice, too."

8

"Oh! I almost forgot
my scarf and hat."

9

"Now, for my jacket.
Hey! I'm all done! I got
dressed all by myself!"

"I must show Mama. She
will be so proud of me!"

"Oh. It's very warm in here. I'll just take off my jacket and hat."

"Now the zipper is stuck!
Help, Mama! Help!"

"Harry, you did a good
job getting dressed for
a cold winter's day...

14

. . . but it's summertime!
Now go out and play in
the warm sunshine!"

For a free color catalog describing Gareth Stevens' list of high-quality children's books, call 1-800-341-3569 (USA) or 1-800-461-9120 (Canada).

Library of Congress Cataloging-in-Publication Data

Gabán, Jesús.
    [Papouf s'habille. English]
    Harry dresses himself / by Jesús Gabán. — North American ed.
        p.   cm. — (Harry the hippo)
    Translation of: Papouf s'habille.
    Summary: Harry the hippo is so pleased to be dressing himself
that he puts on too many clothes.
      ISBN 0-8368-0715-4
      [1. Hippopotamus—Fiction. 2. Clothing and Dress—Fiction.]
    I. Title. II. Series: Gabán, Jesús. Harry the hippo.
PZ7.G1116Har   1991
[E]—dc20   91-12870

North American edition first published in 1992 by

Gareth Stevens Children's Books
1555 North RiverCenter Drive, Suite 201
Milwaukee, Wisconsin 53212, USA

U.S. edition copyright © 1992. Text copyright © 1992 by Gareth Stevens, Inc.
First published in France, copyright © 1990 by Gautier-Languereau.

English text by Eileen Foran
Cover design by Beth Karpfinger and Sharone Burris

Printed in the United States of America

1 2 3 4 5 6 7 8 9 97 96 95 94 93 92